Deerfield Public Library
920 Waukegan Road
Deerfield, IL 60015

DEERFIELD PUBLIC LIBRARY

W9-BFE-649

WITHDRAWN

JUN 0 9 2020

WITHDRAWN

PAPER PLANES

Jim Helmore and Richard Jones

PEACHTREE
ATLANTA

Mia and Ben were the very best of friends.

They lived side by side on the edge of a great, wide lake.

They sailed together...

and swung and sang together.

But what they loved
doing most of all
was making planes.

In the winter, Mia and Ben would race their planes with the geese above.

And in the summer, they would climb into the hills and toss their planes down below, watching them glide home. Mia and Ben were determined to make a plane that could fly all the way across the lake.

But it wasn't mean to be...

Ben had terrible news. He was leaving.
His family was moving to a new home, a long way away.

Mia and Ben were crushed.

How could they stay best friends if they were so far apart?

They promised to never
forget one another,

and they swapped planes
as they said their good-byes.

As the days passed,
Mia missed Ben very much.

She thought of him, way over the sea,
and wondered if he was lonely too.

Winter came again.

But when the geese returned this time,
Mia had no one to race planes with.

Hot tears fell from her eyes.

Mia and Ben would never make a plane that could fly across the lake now.

Mia took the plane Ben had given her and smashed it on the ground. She went to bed, feeling hurt and angry.

That night, as moonlight crept across her bedroom floor,
Mia heard something.

Was it the wind?

No! It was the sound of distant geese
calling and powerful wings beating.

Mia crept out of bed and spied something odd with her telescope in the garden below.

Why, it was the plane she had smashed—as good as new!

Mia hurried outside for a closer look.

The swish and chatter of geese grew louder,
and a wild wind began to blow.

As the wind whipped around Mia's
plane, it grew big enough to climb in.

Suddenly, a huge gust whisked Mia and her enchanted plane into the air.

Up across the lake and away!

Climbing at terrific speed, Mia joined a flock of geese.

Their silver feathers gleamed in the light of the
moon as they rushed through the night.

Up ahead, Mia spotted something familiar in the distance.

Could it be...?

Yes! It was Ben, waving and smiling!
Together they swooped

and skimmed

and soared.

Mia wished she could stay forever,

but as the sun began to rise, she knew it was time to go.

And in the beat of a wing...

Mia woke up and found herself back in her bedroom.

At breakfast time, a package arrived for her.
Inside was a brand new plane—but it had no wings.

There was also a note.

Dear Mia, I really need
your help to finish this.
No one else can make wings
like you!
Love Ben

Mia remembered her dream with Ben and the geese.

Ben might be far away, but that didn't mean Mia had
lost him forever. So she sat down at her table and got to work
on the wings Ben had asked for.

Mia thought of the geese with their long necks stretching and their wide wings beating.

And over the weeks, she worked and she worked and she worked. In the springtime, it was finally ready!

Mia fixed her wings onto the plane Ben had sent her and went down to the water's edge. She threw the plane up into the air, and it...

soared! Higher than any plane she and Ben
had ever made before.

Mia and Ben could still make planes together.
The best planes in the world!

And they would always stay friends.
For now, not even an ocean could keep them apart.

For Phoebe, Émile, and Evan —J. H.

For Toby —R. J.

Published by
PEACHTREE PUBLISHING COMPANY INC.
1700 Chattahoochee Avenue
Atlanta, Georgia 30318-2112
www.peachtree-online.com

Text © 2019 by Jim Helmore
Illustrations © 2019 by Richard Jones

First published in Great Britain in 2019 by Simon and Schuster UK Ltd
1st Floor, 222 Grays Inn Road, London, WC1X 8HB, A CBS Company
First United States version published in 2020 by Peachtree Publishing Company Inc.

All rights reserved. No part of this publication may be reproduced, stored in a retrieval system, or transmitted in any form or by any means—electronic, mechanical, photocopy, recording, or any other—except for brief quotations in printed reviews, without the prior permission of the publisher.

The illustrations were rendered in paint and edited in Adobe Photoshop.

Printed in January 2020 in China
10 9 8 7 6 5 4 3 2 1
First Edition

HC ISBN: 978-1-68263-161-4

Library of Congress Cataloging-in-Publication Data

Names: Helmore, Jim, author. | Jones, Richard, 1977– illustrator.
Title: Paper planes / written by Jim Helmore ; illustrated by Richard Jones.
Description: Atlanta, Georgia : Peachtree Publishing Company Inc., 2020. | "First published in Great Britain in 2019 by Simon and Schuster UK Ltd." | Summary: Neighbors and best friends Mia and Ben love nothing more than making planes and flying them together, but when Ben moves away, both wonder if they can remain friends.
Identifiers: LCCN 2019019546 | ISBN 9781682631614
Subjects: | CYAC: Best friends—Fiction. | Friendship—Fiction. | Paper airplanes—Fiction. | Separation (Psychology)—Fiction.
Classification: LCC PZ7.H375916 Pap 2020 | DDC [E]—dc23 LC record available at *https://lccn.loc.gov/2019019546*